# Let's go Shoolie-Shoo

## CREATIVE ACTIVITIES FOR DANCE AND MUSIC
## AGE 5+

Helen MacGregor and Bobbie Gargrave

D0928295

Illustrated by Carol Jonas
CD produced by Stephen Chadwick
Videoclips filmed by Jamie Acton-Bond

00 864643 09

 AUDIO CD TRACK NUMBERS

VIDEOCLIP NUMBERS

ACC. NO. 86464309 FUND EDUC
LOC. ET CATEGORY CC PRICE £9.99
10 OCT 2007
CLASS No. 792.8 MAC
OXFORD BROOKES
UNIVERSITY LIBRARY

First published 2003
A & C Black (Publishers) Ltd
37 Soho Square, London W1D 3QZ

ISBN 0-7136-6615-3

**All rights reserved.** No part of this publication may be reproduced or used in any form or by any means – photographic, electronic or mechanical, including photocopying, recording, taping or information storage and retrieval systems – without the prior permission in writing of the publishers.

Music text, songs and chants © 2003 Helen MacGregor
Dance text and chants © 2003 Bobbie Gargrave
Illustrations © 2003 Carol Jonas
Edited and developed by Sheena Roberts
Designed by Jocelyn Lucas
Videoclips filmed and produced by Jamie Acton-Bond
CD recorded and mastered by Stephen Chadwick
CD/videoclips compilation © 2003 A & C Black
CD-ROM post-production by Ian Shepherd, SRT
Printed in Great Britain by St Edmundsbury Press Ltd,
Bury St Edmunds, Suffolk

Material referred to in the text as photocopiable, may be photocopied only within an educational establishment and only for the teaching purposes specified in this book.

# CONTENTS

**Shoolie-shoo** African-American playground game

DANCE introducing an imaginative range of movement vocabulary, linked to a game.

MUSIC developing a sense of pulse through physical movement, and on simple instruments.

**Jelly Roll blues** 20th century Jazz

DANCE working with representational movement, stimulated by visual images of underwater creatures.

MUSIC listening and responding to music in jazz/blues style.

**Sounds menu** 21st century processed music

DANCE responding in movement to environmental sounds and showing contrast in action and dynamics.

MUSIC exploring environmental sounds.

**Jarabe tapatio** Mexican band music

DANCE exploring dancing with props, working individually and in small groups.

MUSIC exploring metre of two and three beats in a bar, using body percussion and instruments.

# INTRODUCTION

## THE DANCE ACTIVITIES

These dance activities offer an opportunity for children to explore the basic body actions and to use different parts of their bodies to make the movement. The vocabulary of movement is initiated by a wide range of stimuli, for which the initial starting point is always the music.

The dance work focusses upon the children experiencing, creating and performing short dances that communicate a range of moods, feelings and ideas. Some dances are influenced by specific historical, social or cultural elements.

Each idea creates opportunities for children to be taught a range of specific performance, composition and evaluation skills. They should also develop an awareness and sense of some historical and cultural dance forms.

The activities are flexible and should be tailored to the class needs, but with reference to the appropriate national curriculum. The activities support the process of teaching and learning dance, so that children are given the opportunities to: improvise, explore, select, remember and repeat, develop, practice, refine, perform, and observe.

The music and dance are mutually supportive, but ensure that specific skills are taught which are relevant to the discrete areas of learning.

## THE MUSIC ACTIVITIES

These offer the children a variety of opportunities to explore sounds made with voices, bodies, untuned and tuned percussion, and junk instruments within national curriculum objectives. They can be used alongside a scheme of work to extend children's learning in the areas of performing, listening, appraising and creating music.

As a whole they present a range of musical experiences which will build the vocal, instrumental, improvisation and composition skills of the children, while allowing for differentiation within the activities, eg in Pula, children may chant a simple rhythmic call and response, play untuned percussion to a steady beat or play a repeating pattern on tuned percussion. The musical activities are closely related to the dance ideas but can be explored separately if you wish. They are intended to be flexible — it is not necessary to complete all the activities suggested, and you and the children will have ideas of other ways to develop the music-making, dance and listening.

Recording the children's work at different stages on cassette, CD or video provides further opportunities for listening and appraising, and allows you to track progress.

## USING THE MUSIC RECORDINGS ON THEIR OWN

The twelve pieces of music have been carefully chosen to introduce children to a wide variety of musical styles from different places and times, which will broaden their experience of listening to music. The pieces can be used independently of the suggested activities to give children opportunities to respond spontaneously to what they hear through movement, words or paint. Play a chosen piece (without revealing the title or theme of the linked activities) to explore what the children notice and how they react.

Some children will want to describe their feelings, ideas, likes and dislikes through language, developing their literacy skills, while others will find it easier to express their reactions through other media. Remember that responses will be unique to each child — some may describe pictures they have imagined as they listen, others may recognise an instrument they have heard before, others will not be able to articulate their feelings in words, but may want to move as they listen.

The suggested dance and musical activities lead the children towards more focussed listening and a greater understanding of the music. Through this they will begin to build knowledge and understanding of musical vocabulary and of the musical elements: duration, dynamics, pitch, timbre, texture, tempo and structure.

## THE VIDEOCLIPS

Watch all the videoclips for your own reference before doing the activities.

The videoclips are for both you and for the children to view. Many of the clips show unrehearsed explorations of the activities, performed by teachers and children. They are not final performances, but exemplifications of how you might begin your work together. While these may be of particular use to you, you may also like to show them to the children to stimulate discussion and develop their ideas.

# DANCE AND MUSIC GLOSSARY

## DANCE

**BASIC ACTIONS** – the words used to describe what the body is doing, eg locomotion, turning, jumping, stillness, gesture (see separate definitions below).

**CONTRAST** – movements, shapes, dynamics which are clearly quite different to each other, eg fast v slow, light v heavy, high v low.

**DIRECTION** – moving to the front, back, or to the side.

**DYNAMICS** – a variety of combined qualities used to colour a movement, eg explosive jump, peaceful travelling.

**EXPRESSION** – to perform movements with dynamics and with an understanding of the idea to be communicated.

**GESTURE** – in which a particular part or parts of the body does an action without transferring any weight, eg nod of the head, shrug of the shoulders.

**LEVEL** – the height at which a movement is performed, eg floor, low, middle, high.

**LOCOMOTION** – movement in which the whole body travels.

**MOTIF** – a simple phrase or shape that contains something which can be repeated, varied and developed.

**PHRASE** – a 'sentence' of movement which has a clear shape in time and an ending.

**QUALITY** – a movement's quality is determined by its use of time (fast/slow), weight (light/heavy), flow (bound/free), space (direct/flexible).

**REPRESENT** – to interpret through movement an animal, idea or character as opposed to miming the action or 'pretending to be'.

**SEQUENCE** – one movement followed by another leading to patterns of movement.

**SHAPE** – achieved when the body holds and maintains a position in space.

**STILLNESS** – in which the whole body pauses motionless.

## THE ARTISTIC PROCESS

**DEVELOP** – altering the action, space, time, or quality of movements to build longer phrases, extend motifs and construct sections or whole dances.

**EXPLORE** – exploring movement imaginatively in response to guided tasks.

**FORMATION** – the organisation of bodies (dancers) in space to create different designs, eg circle/line, eg Time line.

**IMPROVISE** – immediate or unplanned response to a stimulus or task.

**REFINE** – to practise and remember movement in order to improve it.

**STRUCTURE** – the form of a whole dance which organises the movement, phrases or motifs into a complete dance, eg narrative storytelling as in Dragon hunt.

**TYPE** – a broad classification of dances:
  *abstract dance*, eg Sorbet (based in movement itself)
  *comic dance*, eg Jelly Roll Blue Seas (depicting humour)
  *dance drama/narrative dance*, eg Dragon hunt (a storytelling dance)
  *dramatic dance*, eg Twister (use of character and relationships)
  *traditional dance*, eg Stick tricks (roots of dance in culture and tradition)

## MUSIC

**DURATION** – the word used in music to refer to the length of a sound or silence.

**DYNAMICS** – the volume of music, usually described in terms of loud/quiet.

**PITCH** – refers to the complete range of sounds in music from the lowest to the highest.

**RHYTHM** – patterns of long and short played within a steady beat.

**TEMPO** – the speed of music, usually described in terms of fast/slow.

**TEXTURE** – layers of sound, eg the two layers of sound created by a melody accompanied by a drum beat.

**TIMBRE** – quality of sound, eg squeaky. All instruments, including voices, have a particular sound quality which are referred to as timbre.

# LET'S GO SHOOLIE-SHOO

**Shoolie-shoo** is an African-American playground game. Individual children choose a travelling idea – flying, swimming, rowing – which they take turns to perform, travelling round the outside of a circle formed by the other children.

## Dance objectives
- Work within the formation of a circle.
- Perform dance actions in an order, and in time with a steady beat.

## Music objectives
- Invent actions and select sounds made on percussion instruments.
- Perform to a steady beat.

## Resources
- Travelling word cards.
- Selection of percussion instruments, eg maracas, tambourines, cymbals, xylophone.

## Preparation

Sing the song together, using CD track 1 to learn the melody and words.

Watch the videoclip alone or with the children to familiarise yourselves with the structure of the game.

Collect suggestions from every child for travelling movements and write them onto separate cards. Some ideas are given opposite.

---

Just from the kitchen,

shoolie-shoo,

With a handful of cookies,

shoolie-shoo,

O, dear Daniel*,

shoolie-shoo,

Fly away over yonder,

shoolie-shoo.

*Stand in a circle and clap the beat. One child 'flies' around outside the circle.*

*On 'Daniel' the first child stands behind Daniel and taps the beat with both hands on Daniel's shoulders.*

Just from the kitchen,

shoolie-shoo,

With a handful of cookies,

shoolie-shoo,

O, dear Sarah*,

shoolie-shoo,

Fly away over yonder,

shoolie-shoo.

*Daniel 'flies' around the circle and the first child takes his place.*

*Daniel stops behind a new player and the game repeats.*

*substitute child's real name

ski

fly

skate

swim

paddle

row

drive

jump

bounce

skip

## DANCE EXPLORATION

- Remind the children of the flying idea in *Shoolie-shoo*. Ask them to suggest other travelling ideas, eg swimming, skiing, rowing, sailing, skating, galloping, etc.
- Call out one of the travelling ideas. The children respond to it in an improvisational way (unplanned) showing their own interpretation and using the whole of the general space.
- Encourage the children to represent the image of the word in the qualities of their movement, eg

  **swim** – strong, direct and smooth arm gestures;

  **row** – sharp, strong movements leaning forwards and backwards;

  **skate** – long, smooth, continuous movement with stretches and slides.

- Stand in a circle and practise the travelling actions on the spot, noting interesting interpretations.

## MUSIC EXPLORATION

- Play the game and sing the song as described and prepared on page 6 - repeat the flying action until the game is well established.
- Stand in a circle to play the game again. This time, the travelling cards are placed face down in the centre of the ring. The child who begins the game picks a card and shows it to the others, eg swim. The circle children sing the song and make the matching movement on the spot while the travelling child moves around the outside of the circle.
- The travelling child, stands behind 'Remi', who will choose the next card and continue the game:

### Swimming child begins:

Just from the kitchen,
　shoolie-shoo,
With a handful of cookies,
　shoolie-shoo,
Oh dear, Remi,
　shoolie-shoo,
**Swim** away over yonder,
　shoolie-shoo.

## MUSIC DEVELOPMENT

- Divide into small groups and allocate one travelling word card to each group. Ask the groups to explore and choose sounds on instruments to represent their word. Encourage them to think carefully about methods of playing their chosen instruments to produce matching sounds, eg

  **fly** – tap a suspended cymbal in long, soft strokes;

  **swim** – shake maracas in an arc to make long sounds;

  **ski** – sweep fingertips across a tambourine skin;

  **row** – slide a pair of soft beaters up and down a xylophone using both hands.

- Give each group practice at playing their instruments in the chosen method while everyone else sings the song to these words:

> Just from the kitchen,
>> shoolie-shoo,
> With a handful of cookies,
>> shoolie-shoo,
> Oh, musicians,
>> shoolie-shoo,
> **Play** away over yonder,
>> shoolie-shoo.

- Help the children to play their movement sound within the steady beat of the song, eg running sounds will fall on every beat, while swimming sounds might fall on every fourth beat.

- Sing the song again. This time, select the order in which the groups play by holding up a travelling card between each repeat of the song, eg swimming card is selected –

> **Swimming group plays:**

> Just from the kitchen,
>> shoolie-shoo,
> With a handful of cookies,
>> shoolie-shoo,
> Oh, musicians,
>> shoolie-shoo,
> **Swim** away over yonder,
>> shoolie-shoo.

> (display the next card and continue)

- As a class, discuss a planned order of verses, eg starting with the quietest and ending with the loudest, or choosing a sequence of contrasting timbres.

- Place the cards in the chosen sequence where everyone can see them, then perform all of the verses as each group accompanies.

## DANCE DEVELOPMENT

- Divide into small groups, each with a travelling card (stay in the same groups from the music development or try a new travelling action).

- As a class, identify the order in which the groups will perform their travelling actions. The order should allow the movement to build from verse to verse – beginning with the lightest or slowest movements and going to the strongest or fastest movements, eg

| swim | row | work | run |
|------|-----|------|-----|

- Invite a child from each group to perform the movements in the chosen order to check that the sequence builds as planned.

- Give each group practice in performing their movement within the steady beat, while the others sing, then perform the whole sequence.

## PERFORMANCE

- Divide into small groups as in the developments and prepare a sequence of movements and music to perform together in a large space. Display the travelling cards where everyone can see them and make sure that the groups are clear about the order.

- Each group comprises:

  **musicians and singers**, sitting together in their groups, which are positioned in separate areas of the space

  **dancers**, who will use the whole space and will individually perform all of the movements of each verse.

- The singers and musicians accompany the dancers in the chosen order.

# JELLY ROLL BLUE SEAS

***Jelly Roll Blues*** **is a piece of jazz music by Louis Armstrong which features trumpet, trombone, piano, clarinet and percussion.**

## Dance objectives
- Use different body shapes in both movement and stillness.
- Perform basic dance actions with appropriate qualities in relation to an idea.
- Move in and around the space safely.

## Music objectives
- Recognise individual instruments played in a jazz/blues style.
- Make simple instruments to accompany the recording.

## Resources
- Home-made instrument materials (see illustrations on page 13) from which to make:
    ***simple-cymbal*** – aluminium foil plate tapped with a teaspoon;
    ***plinky-piano*** – stretch several rubber bands in parallel round a strong, open-topped, card box; pluck with fingertips;
    ***tootly-trumpet*** – push a cardboard cone (the trumpet bell) into one end of a tube of card; wind tape round the other end to make a mouthpiece to toot through;
    ***classy-clarinet*** – hum or sing through a length of hollow plastic pipe on which finger holes or keys are drawn or stuck on.

## Preparation

Show the children the videoclip of underwater creatures, and talk about the way they move, in order to build a vocabulary for dance exploration.
As a class, prepare the home-made instruments.

## DANCE EXPLORATION

### 2 JELLY ROLL BLUES

Discuss the different underwater creatures illustrated on pages 10-11 – the fish, jellyfish and octopus. Explain that you are all going to go on an imaginary underwater journey where you will see these creatures.

Play the CD. As the children listen, guide them verbally and visually through the imaginary journey, referring to the illustration and videoclips.

• Find a large space and begin to explore the movement actions of the underwater creatures.

**Fish**
– travelling lightly and quickly in and out of spaces, using curved pathways, stopping and swaying while using hands and arms like fins to ripple from side to side;

– using vocabulary to extend the children's responses, eg dart, shimmer, flick, weave, glide, quiver.

**Jellyfish**
– bobbing around the space making light, gentle, floating movements;

– stopping and wobbling the whole body whilst moving slowly up and down and around in their own personal space;

– using vocabulary to extend the children's responses, eg fan, glide, rotate, float, trail.

**Octopus**
– balancing on hands and feet, explore moving around space by stretching arms and legs out and placing them in new space; make the body parts move successively, one after the other;

– stopping and stretching body parts away from the centre of the body, and curling them back in towards it;

– using vocabulary to extend the children's responses, eg curling, stretching, twisting, wrapping, gathering, turning.

## MUSIC EXPLORATION

### 2 JELLY ROLL BLUES

Ask the children to play any imaginary musical instrument they like as they listen to the music.

Ask them questions about what they played and noticed in the music, eg

• Which instruments did you hear? (They may have recognised some of these: trumpet, trombone, piano, clarinet, drum kit/ hi hat cymbal.)

• Was the music fast or slow? (Slow.)

• Do you know what this type of music is called? (Jazz, or blues.)

Show the children the pictures of the instruments (on pages 10-11) and watch the video clips of the children miming playing.

• What do they notice in the pictures, about the difference between the ways the trumpet and trombone are played? (The trumpet has three keys which are pressed, the trombone has a slide which moves up and down to make the notes higher or lower.)

• How is the clarinet played in the picture? (Like a recorder, using the fingers of both hands to change the notes.)

### 2 JELLY ROLL BLUES

Ask the children to join in with the music by miming the featured instruments as they hear them (the piano and cymbals accompany throughout):

| | |
|---|---|
| Trumpet melody/ trombone slides | 0.00 – 0.40 |
| Piano low stabs alternating with high tremolos | 0.40 |
| Clarinet melody | 0.55 |
| Trumpet melody | 1.28 |
| Piano low stabs/ high tremolos | 2.00 |
| All | 2.18 – end |

• Did they recognise the changes of instruments?

• Did some children notice the trombone slides?

• Did some children recognise the clarinet when it played the melody?

- Did they move to match the tempo of the music?
- How did they represent the low piano stabs and high tremolos? (eg by using both hands and moving from left to right; by making short, sharp movements followed by shaking fingers in the air.)

 **JELLY ROLL BLUES**

Have a 'jam session'. Make the class into a jazz band, allocating one instrument to each child and asking them to mime as they hear their instrument played.

## DANCE DEVELOPMENT

 **JELLY ROLL BLUES**

The children use the movements already explored to interpret the different underwater creatures as their corresponding instruments are played:

    fish – trumpet/trombone

    jellyfish – piano

    octopus – clarinet

Encourage the children to improve the quality of their movements by listening and responding carefully to the music.

- To develop the dance further, work in pairs and try to lead and follow each other when performing the different underwater creatures.

## MUSIC DEVELOPMENT

- Choose a small group to play along with the CD using the home-made instruments (page 10). The cymbals should play throughout, while the others join in only when they hear their matching instrument, as explored above. All play during the last section.

## PERFORMANCE

 **JELLY ROLL BLUES**

Perform the dance with the CD and the accompanying home-made jazz band music. The children choose whether to be musicians or dancers.

# SOUNDS MENU

**Sounds menu is a piece of 21st century music by Stephen Chadwick. He uses real recordings of kitchen implements and equipment and processes them digitally to create a lively texture of sounds and rhythms.**

## Dance objectives

- Respond to sounds using a variety of different parts of the body.
- Explore gesture in movement.
- Use a range of different qualities of movement.

## Music objectives

- Recognise and identify environmental sounds.
- Improvise vocal and instrumental sounds in response to pictures to create a chance sequence of sounds.

## Resources

- Kitchen sound cards (see opposite).
- Sounds menu die (see template right).
- Instruments.

## Preparation

Copy and paste the six kitchen illustrations onto separate cards. These are the items of equipment which are featured in Sounds menu. Show the cards to the children and discuss the kinds of sounds the children would expect them to make:

  tap
  kettle
  bottle opener
  spin dryer
  cutlery drawer
  plug

Follow the instructions for making a Sounds menu die (opposite).

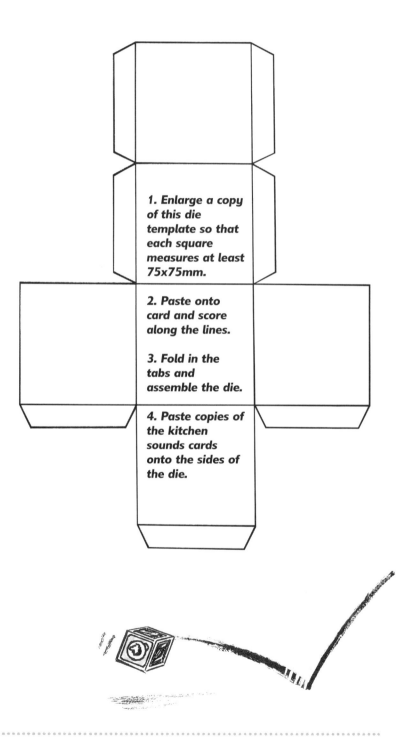

*1. Enlarge a copy of this die template so that each square measures at least 75x75mm.*

*2. Paste onto card and score along the lines.*

*3. Fold in the tabs and assemble the die.*

*4. Paste copies of the kitchen sounds cards onto the sides of the die.*

## MUSIC EXPLORATION

**③ SOUNDS MENU**

Tell the children they will hear a piece of music which is made from real sounds recorded in the home. Ask them to listen carefully. Which sounds did they recognise? (eg dripping tap, spin dryer, whistling kettle.)

Listen again to check the identity of the sounds.

• Invite individuals to make sounds with their voices to match the kitchen sounds – the class copy.

**③ SOUNDS MENU**

Listen to the CD, then ask the children to describe some of the sounds they heard in more detail, eg

dripping tap – short quiet sounds which play a tune

spin dryer – speeds up then slows down

kettle – a long hissing sound which becomes higher

cutlery drawer – short, bright sounds which play a rhythm

cork – three loud, short sounds

plug – a low, glugging sound

They may also notice a vacuum cleaner, water running down the drain, a toaster popping up, a washing machine and a microwave ping.

**④ SOUNDS MENU SOUNDS**

Place the kitchen sounds cards (page 15) where all the children can see them.

Listen to the CD. Invite a child to point to each sound card as they notice it during the music.

Ask:

Which sounds were heard only once? (Kettle and spin dryer.)

Which sound card was heard first? (Dripping tap.)

Which sound was heard most often? (Cork.)

## DANCE EXPLORATION

Explore the following movements, while sitting down, using arms  and upper body:

**dripping tap** – begin with both arms stretched high towards the ceiling. Explore sharp, jerky, staccato movement alternatively pull the arms down towards the floor bit by bit. The movement will take a vertical line down;

**spin dryer** – explore continuous rotational movement which changes in speed: slow to fast – fast to slow. There should be a clear acceleration and deceleration in response to the sound, eg rolling arms around each other;

**kettle** – explore movement which begins low and rises, also beginning small and expanding in size. The movement should be continuous as it increases in level and size;

**cutlery drawer** – explore free, vigorous movement by shaking different parts of the body in response to the sound 'shake, rattle and roll'. As the sound stops, the movement should also stop. This should be repetitive and very energetic;

**cork** – explore direct short, sharp movements which follow a change in level. The movement could be three consecutive actions as if the cork is being pulled from the bottle; go – stop, go – stop, pull out (the biggest movement, is the final one);

**plug** – place one hand over the top of another, pull one hand away as if to release the plug.

## MUSIC DEVELOPMENT

• Using a range of instruments and soundmakers, help the children  find sounds to match the kitchen sounds in *Sounds menu*, eg

**dripping tap** – wooden temple block;

**spin dryer** – cymbal and metal brush;

**kettle** – swanee whistle or recorder head;

**cutlery drawer** – jingle ring;

**cork** – bass xylophone;

**plug** – tap cardboard tube end, blow bubbles in water bottle.

• As a class, find a way of playing each chosen instrument to make a pattern which can be remembered and repeated, eg

**cutlery drawer** – extend jingle ring and draw it back into the body while shaking x 3;

**cork** – short, sharp, quiet scrape, louder scrape, loud cheek pop.

• Now play this *Sounds menu* game. You will need two or three sets of the kitchen sounds cards (page 15) and a large *Sounds menu* die (see template and instructions page 14).

Pass the die around as you all chant:

> ## Six sounds, a game of chance,
> ## Sounds to make a kitchen dance.

The child who is holding the die at the end of the chant rolls it on the floor to select a sound. The child picks out the matching kitchen sound card and uses it to conduct the class: when the card is raised for all to see, they improvise matching sounds using their voices. The conductor gives a stop signal by turning the card onto its blank side, placing it where everyone can see.

Repeat the chant until six sounds have been chosen in this way (some of the sounds may be repeated in the sequence of six, and some may not have been selected).

Now choose a conductor to lead the class in a performance of the complete sequence by pointing to the cards one by one. The conductor may choose how long each of the sounds continues before moving to the next.

Record the performance, then listen and discuss what the children liked about the chance sequence created by rolling the die. What would they change if they were choosing the order themselves?

## DANCE DEVELOPMENT

• Develop the explored upper body actions and gestures into whole body movements:

**dripping tap** – develop by using other parts of the body to make short, sharp movements;

**spin dryer** – develop turning movements by finding other ways to turn and spin using different parts of the body – try accelerating and decelerating;

**kettle** – develop by using whole body stretches, moving from a curled to a stretched shape;

**cutlery drawer** – develop by shaking whole body whilst moving forwards and backwards in a repetitive way;

**cork** – develop by enlarging the strong arm movement into jumping actions;

**plug** – develop whole body rotational, sinking movement as if water is swirling its way down the pipe.

## DANCE AND MUSIC DEVELOPMENT

• For each kitchen sound pattern developed earlier, build a short rhythmic dance sequence to match, eg

**knife drawer** – shake shake shake and freeze, or forwards backwards x 3;
**cork** – jump low/jump higher/explosive jump.

• Perform these, adding the vocal sounds.

## PERFORMANCE

• Play the Sounds menu game to find a chance order of sounds. As a whole class, perform the order using vocal sounds and movement. Choose a conductor to point to the cards in the order of performance. The performers change to the next sound and movement when the conductor indicates.

# DUST BUSTERS

**Dust busters** uses a lively piece of Mexican band music, **Jarabe Tapatio**, which features the trumpet. The music has a metre of two and three beats in a bar during the first and third sections (A), and three beats in a bar in the middle section (B).

## Dance objectives
- Work with props.
- Develop a simple motif in pairs and small groups.
- Respond to a change of metre from two to three beats in a bar and from three to two.

## Music objectives
- Explore metre of two and three beats in a bar.
- Explore ternary structure (ABA).
- Perform music with a metre of two and three.

## Resources
- Household props:
  dusters, feather dusters, scrubbing brushes, rubber gloves.
- A selection of percussion instruments.

## Preparation
Discuss household chores and show the children the props. Identify possible working actions with each – scrubbing with the scrubbing brush, wiping and polishing with the cloth, etc.

Explore vocal sounds to match the working actions, eg
  **scrubbing brush** – ch ch ch ch ch ch...
  **feather duster** – flick flick...

rub shake scrub slide

# B                                              A

squeeze flick dab push wring polish shake pull

## DANCE EXPLORATION

- Give each child a prop:

- Remind the children of the working actions they identified during the preparation.

**⑤ JARABE TAPATIO – SECTION A**

Improvise a variety of working actions using the props. Encourage the children to respond to the speed and beat of the music (1 2 1 2 ...).

Create opportunities for the children to explore a variety of actions. This may be done by pausing the music and giving the children time to swap props.

- Each child, working with a prop, now selects a simple working action which they can remember and repeat in time with the music.

- Remind children that they can use a variety of different levels and directions to develop their working action, eg the feather duster might be flicked high then low.

**⑤ JARABE TAPATIO – SECTION A**

The children perform the working actions individually with the music, moving on the beat (1 2 1 2 ...).

- Develop the working actions in small groups. All the children in each group have the same prop and the group chooses one action to perform together.

**⑤ JARABE TAPATIO – SECTION A**

Perform the selected working actions as a group with the music, moving on the beat.

## MUSIC EXPLORATION

**⑤ JARABE TAPATIO – SECTION A**

Encourage the children to tap the beat on alternate knees as they listen to section A (see first part of videoclip).

Listen again, finding a way to keep the beat with different parts of the body, eg

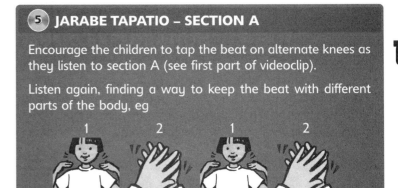

- Remind the children of the actions and vocal sounds they identified in the preparation.

- Divide the children into four groups. Each group selects an instrument and sound to match one household prop. Find a way to play the instrument to make a two-beat pattern as they did when they chose body percussion above, eg

**duster:** tambour – rub fingertips clockwise then anticlockwise around the drum skin;

**scrubbing brush:** guiro – scrape backwards then forwards;

**feather duster:** bells – shake high then low;

**rubber gloves:** shakers – swish left then right.

**⑤ JARABE TAPATIO – SECTION A**

Give each group a turn to play the chosen sounds to the music, matching the beat of 1 2 1 2.

- Give each group a turn to play their pattern without the music. To help the groups keep a steady beat, conduct them by performing their action with the appropriate prop.

- Select one child from each group to conduct the players with their action and prop. All the groups now play together, maintaining the steady beat.

## DANCE DEVELOPMENT

### ⑥ JARABE TAPATIO – SECTIONS A AND B

In the groups they formed in the dance exploration, the children perform their working actions to the music. Explain that they should stop and hold a stillness when they hear a change in the music (the beginning of the B section which changes to a metre of three beats in a bar).

Play the B section again, encouraging the children to move individually, using the whole space, in response to the changed quality and metre of the music. Practise:

> travelling – moving in fluid, free-flowing, abstract ways, using the props as dance partners in a playful, imaginative way;

> working in groups – after travelling, the children meet in groups of threes, fours and fives with similar props and move in response to the new metre, continuing to use the props as dance partners within the group.

Perform the B section as a choreographed whole: travelling – group work – travelling back to be ready for the start of the A section again.

## MUSIC DEVELOPMENT

### ⑥ JARABE TAPATIO – SECTIONS A AND B

Encourage the children to tap the beat again on alternate knees as they listen to section A.

At the beginning of the B section, the children change to a pattern of three beats to the bar, eg

Listen to section B again, finding a new way to keep a metre of three beats by performing a pattern with different parts of the body, eg shoulders clap clap, shoulders clap clap ...

- Now choose a small group to play chime bars:

(Encourage the children to bounce the beater gently in the centre of each bar to make a ringing sound. An alternative pattern, shown on the videoclip, is C G G  C G G...)

- While the chime bar group play this pattern, the other children perform the body percussion patterns they found.

- As an extension, some chime bar players may be able to alternate between the pattern of two and three beats to provide an accompaniment for the children to perform the corresponding action patterns.

## PERFORMANCE

### ⑦ JARABE TAPATIO – COMPLETE

Listen to the whole piece of music and identify the structure. Explain that this music is like a musical sandwich:

A bread     B jam     A bread

Perform the dance using the structure:

A: small groups performing working actions in unison

B: individual then group responses with props as partner

A: repeat

- In the instrumental groups from the exploration and development, perform a piece of music in ABA structure. Copy the illustration of the ABA sections (page 19). Use this as a graphic score to conduct the changes of section.

- With the illustration placed where it can be seen easily, point to the sections in turn to direct the players:

A: four groups with conductors perform instrumental patterns in a two beat metre;

B: chime bar players perform in three-beat metre;

A: repeat.

- For a final performance, decide whether to use the CD or the children's own music as an accompaniment to the dance.

# TWISTER

*Sumer is icumen in* by Robert Saxton is from a set of 20th century variations by nineteen contemporary British composers, who have used the medieval song of the same name as their inspiration. This variation brings summer in with a storm – giving the Twister activities their theme.

## Dance objectives
- Explore a range of movements suitable to an idea.
- Perform dance actions with appropriate dynamics for the idea.
- Work in small groups, using circular formations.

## Music objectives
- Select descriptive sounds.
- Improvise changes in volume (loud and quiet) and tempi (speeds) in response to a conductor.

## Resources
- Gymnastic ribbons or scarves.
- Storm soundmakers, eg biscuit tins, junk metal, cardboard boxes and a selection of beaters.

## Preparation

Show the children the videoclip of an American tornado (twister) to identify its characteristics, eg
> funnel shape
> movement across the land
> twisting and turning
> power and speed

## DANCE EXPLORATION

### 8 SUMER IS ICUMEN IN

Listen to the music and imagine the twister approaching.

Ask:

How does the music make you feel? (Excited, fearful, restless ...)
What movements could we use in dance to show the twister? (Turning, twisting, swirling, spinning, leaping ...)

Invite the children to explore a variety of twister actions as they listen to the music again. Use different parts of the body to turn on and around.

Develop the exploration by increasing the size of the actions from small to large, and the speed from slow to fast.

Further develop the actions by incorporating them into travelling actions, so that the children experiment with advancing and retreating, changing direction, pausing then moving forward again.

(When exploring turning, ensure that the children avoid dizziness by changing the direction of turn, by resting between turns and by interposing other actions such as jumping.)

## MUSIC EXPLORATION

### 8 SUMER IS ICUMEN IN

Remind the children of the videoclip of a twister. Listen to the music, explaining that it describes a summer storm. Ask the children to describe it, eg

　it turns;

　it's fast and loud;

　it climbs up, the sounds get higher.

- Discuss the sounds you might hear if you were in a twister: windows rattling, doors banging, breaking glass, objects lifted up into the air then crashing down.

- Choose instruments and soundmakers to describe these effects, eg

　**junk metal** – hubcaps, metal sheets

　**biscuit tins** filled with buttons

　**cardboard boxes** and **wooden beaters**

　**wobble boards**

　**recorder tops** or **whistle sirens**

　**shakers**

- Choose a child to conduct the others by moving their arms in circles to show when the twister starts, when it grows stronger and when it dies down.

The others play freely (not observing a steady beat, and not necessarily playing continuously), responding to the conductor by increasing the volume and speed of their playing.

## DANCE DEVELOPMENT

- Work in groups of four to six, with or without joined hands, exploring what a circle can do, eg turn around, move in and out, change level.

- Develop the twister movements in these groups, using the circle formation as a basis. Use turning and travelling movements within a zoned area to develop a group dance which shows the twister building up, reaching a climax and dying down. (The videoclip shows a large group working with spirals.)

- To develop the movement further, gymnastic ribbons or scarves could be used to create spiralling, circling, twisting air patterns.

- Work on the qualities of the movement to interpret the menacing and violent actions of the twister.

## MUSIC DEVELOPMENT

- Divide into four groups or 'farmhouses', each in its own space. Give each group a set of instruments from the sounds explored earlier.

- Rehearse each group playing their sounds in turn. Appoint a conductor who will direct the group to play by approaching it, moving round it, then moving away as if a twister were approaching then leaving their farmhouse. As in the exploration, the children respond by creating a build up and dying away in the volume of their sound.

## PERFORMANCE

- As in the music development, farmhouse groups of musicians and dancers are situated in their own separate space – their farmhouses.

- Choose a conductor to be the 'twister'. As the twister moves towards a farmhouse, the players will begin to make their storm sounds while the dancers respond with their group dance.

- To create a complete performance, the groups respond in turn to the twister conductor's approach and arrival. Each finds itself at the centre of the storm until the twister moves on to menace another farmhouse.

# THE GRASSHOPPERS DANCE

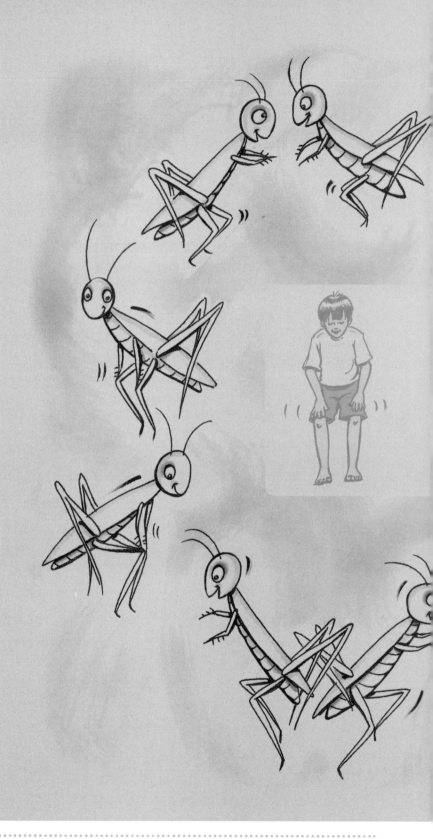

*The grasshopper's dance* is a piece of light, entertaining orchestral music, composed by Ernest Buccalossi in 1905. As with many other pieces of music of this era the theme is illustrated humorously by the instruments. In this case the guiro plays a rhythm representing the grasshopper's chirping, while a glockenspiel plays a jaunty grasshopper dance melody.

## Dance objectives
- Remember and repeat a given action sequence.
- Work in a variety of ways with a partner.
- Improve footwork and rhythm skills.

## Music objectives
- Perform an action song.
- Accompany an action song with simple ostinatos.
- Select sounds to make an arrangement of the song.

## Resources
- Glockenspiel notes: E♭ and E♭'.
- Guiros.
- A selection of untuned percussion.

## Preparation

Make yourself familiar with the song and with the dance steps, using track 9 and videoclip 22.

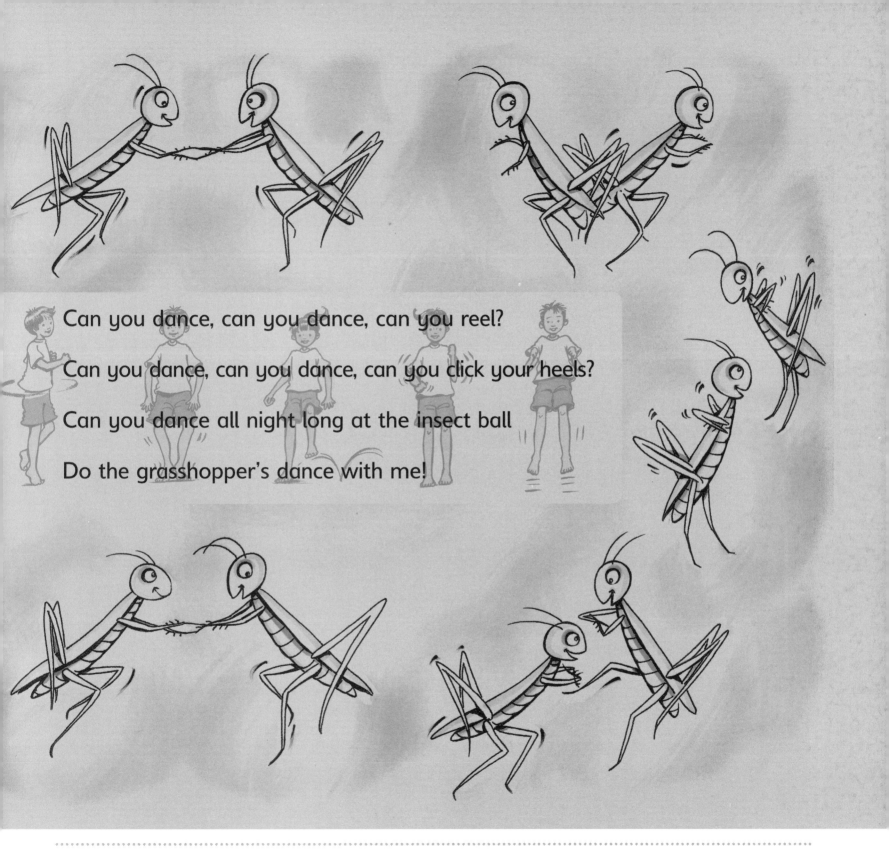

Can you dance, can you dance, can you reel?

Can you dance, can you dance, can you click your heels?

Can you dance all night long at the insect ball

Do the grasshopper's dance with me!

## 9-10 THE GRASSHOPPER'S SONG

Learn the grasshopper's song by singing it with track 9, joining in as it becomes familiar:

> Can you dance, can you dance, can you reel?
>
> Can you dance, can you dance, can you click your heels?
>
> Can you dance all night long at the insect ball
>
> Do the grasshopper dance with me!

Perform the song to the backing track (10).

## 11 THE GRASSHOPPER'S SONG

Teach the children the dance actions which accompany *The Grasshopper's song*. Use CD track 11 which has a caller:

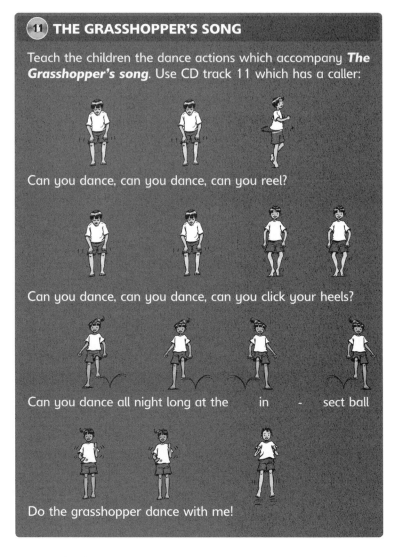

Can you dance, can you dance, can you reel?

Can you dance, can you dance, can you click your heels?

Can you dance all night long at the     in  -  sect ball

Do the grasshopper dance with me!

• Give the children time to practise the dance pattern so that they can remember and repeat it with confidence.

## 12 THE GRASSHOPPER'S DANCE – FIRST SECTION CALLED

When the dance pattern learned above is secure, perform it to the orchestral music, which is a little faster than the sung version. The pattern is repeated.

## DANCE DEVELOPMENT

> **13** **THE GRASSHOPPER'S DANCE** – MIDDLE SECTION
>
> As they listen to the middle section, the children work individually on different travelling steps in time to the music – walk, jog, skip, jump, hop, side-step, etc.
>
> Try using different directions whilst travelling to create different pathways – forwards, backwards, sideways, zigzag, straight, curved.
>
> Using the music again, pairs of children work together to explore:
> - a range of turning actions
> - do-si-do
> - greeting each other in different ways
> - swinging partner

- Ask the children to choose three favourite travelling actions to perform in sequence, eg side-step – hopscotch – skip.

- Practise calling these travelling actions, counting three groups of eight beats, eg

| 1 | 2 | 3 | 4 | 5 | 6 | 7 | 8 |
|---|---|---|---|---|---|---|---|
| travel | 2 | 3 | 4 | 5 | 6 | 7 | 8 |
| travel | 2 | 3 | 4 | 5 | 6 | 7 | 8 |
| travel | 2 | 3 | 4 | 5 | 6 | 7 | 8 |

- Let the children in pairs choose three of their partner movements to create a sequence. Call three groups of eight again for them:

| together | 2 | 3 | 4 | 5 | 6 | 7 | 8 |
|---|---|---|---|---|---|---|---|
| together | 2 | 3 | 4 | 5 | 6 | 7 | 8 |
| together | 2 | 3 | 4 | 5 | 6 | 7 | 8 |

- Practise a complete sequence. Include four counts for the children to find a partner.

| travel | 2 | 3 | 4 | 5 | 6 | 7 | 8 |
|---|---|---|---|---|---|---|---|
| travel again | | 3 | 4 | 5 | 6 | 7 | 8 |
| travel again | | 3 | 4 | 5 | 6 | 7 | 8 |
| find a partner | | 3 | 4 | | | | |
| together | 2 | 3 | 4 | 5 | 6 | 7 | 8 |
| together again | | 3 | 4 | 5 | 6 | 7 | 8 |
| together again | | 3 | 4 | 5 | 6 | 7 | 8 |

> **14** **THE GRASSHOPPER'S DANCE** – ABA CALLED
>
> Perform the complete dance to track 14. You will hear a caller giving instructions.

## MUSIC DEVELOPMENT

- Choose a small group to play the glockenspiel ostinato accompaniment heard on *The Grasshopper's song* (track 9):

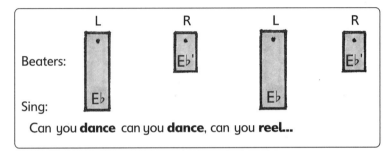

- Choose a small group to play the rhythmic ostinato on guiros (scrapers), using these words to help the players:

- Combine this with the glockenspiel accompaniment, deciding when to add the guiros and the number of repeats of the pattern.

- Play the glockenspiel ostinato twice as an introduction then continue it throughout the song.

- If appropriate, add other insect sound effects, eg

  **butterfly** – Indian bells,
  **ladybirds** – small castanets,
  **bees** – kazoos.

- Make an arrangement of the whole piece, combining the ostinatos and extra instrumental ideas with the song.

## PERFORMANCE

Create a complete performance of dance and music consisting of the song and its accompaniment, followed by the dance accompanied by the CD (called or music only). Use the introduction on the orchestral version (tracks 12-14: 00–00:11) to move into positions for the dance.

# SORBET

*Sorbet no 2* by Evelyn Glennie is an improvised piece of music performed on a pair of small Chinese cymbals. The performer explores and uses many different playing techniques to produce a colourful range of sounds.

## Dance objectives
- Listen and respond to sounds.
- Use a variety of basic actions, eg travelling, turning, jumping.
- Work in pairs using action and reaction.

## Music objectives
- Explore the range of sounds and techniques of playing cymbals.
- Improvise sounds to lead a dancer in a performance.

## Resources
- Pairs of hand-held cymbals or Indian bells.

## Preparation

View the videoclip of a cymbal and dance improvisation on your own or with the children.

Before introducing a pair of cymbals to the children, explore the range of sounds which you can make on them yourself, using different playing techniques.

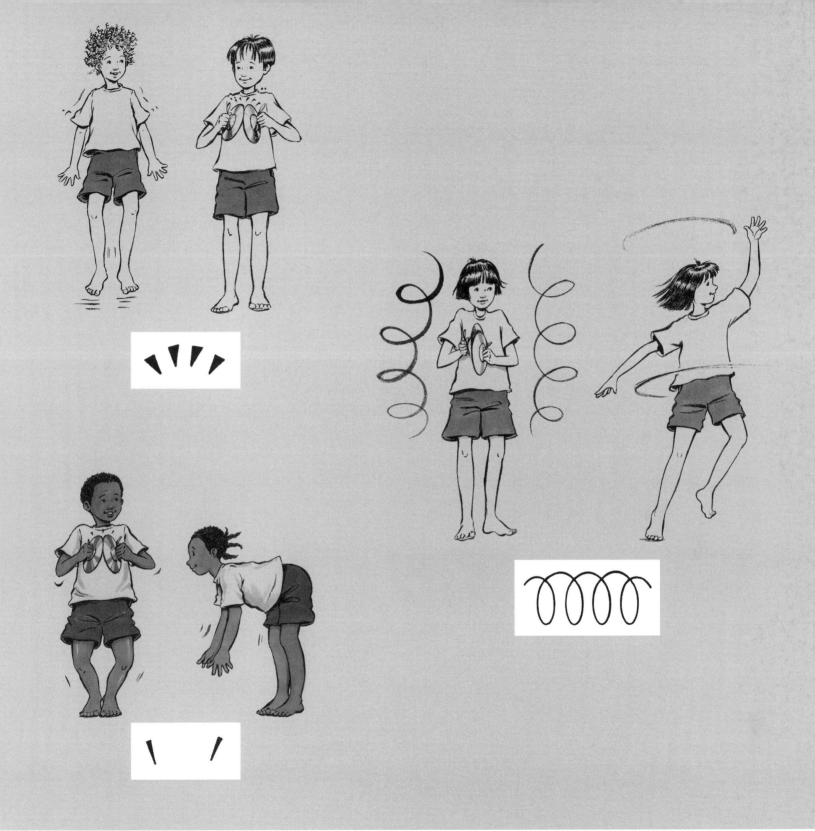

## DANCE EXPLORATION

- Standing in a circle, the children perform any movement they choose, one after the other.

- Repeat. This time the children (with help if needed) each describe the movement they have made, eg

  – it was long and wiggly;

  – it was short and fast;

  – it was a wide stretch.

### ⑯ SORBET

As they listen to the CD, the children individually respond in movement to each of the different sounds they hear.

Encourage them to move at the same time as they hear each sound, noticing and responding to the changes.

Listen again and talk about the quality of the sounds and how this may affect the performance of the dance actions, eg

> long sound – stretched movement
>
> short sound – sharp/staccato movement
>
> fast/slow sound – increase or decrease of speed
>
> quiet sound – soft movement
>
> loud sound – strong movement
>
> starting and stopping sounds – pause or hesitate

Perform the improvisation again. Encourage the children to pay attention to the quality of their movements in response to the quality of the sounds.

## MUSIC EXPLORATION

- You will need one pair of small metal cymbals or Indian bells.

- Sit the children in a circle and explain that each child will have a turn at finding one way of playing the cymbals. Demonstrate holding the cymbals by the handles or string.

- Now pass the cymbals to the first child, who finds a way of making a sound. Continue round the circle until each child has had a turn.

- Repeat, asking the children to describe differences in the sounds made, eg

  loud or quiet – long or short  – tapping, sliding, clashing together – gentle – strong …

### ⑯ SORBET

Now listen to the CD, asking the children to notice the different sounds they hear.

Can they identify:

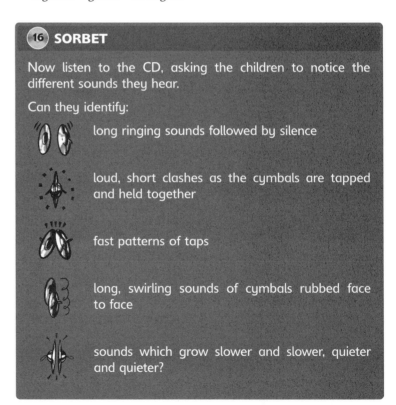

long ringing sounds followed by silence

loud, short clashes as the cymbals are tapped and held together

fast patterns of taps

long, swirling sounds of cymbals rubbed face to face

sounds which grow slower and slower, quieter and quieter?

- Play the circle game again. This time ask each child to choose one of the sounds and methods of playing they heard in the music.

## MUSIC DEVELOPMENT

- Show the children the graphic notations in the illustration (p30-31) to remind them of the different cymbal sounds they have explored.
- Choose one of the children to play any of the sounds in their own improvised sequence.
- Give other children the opportunity to improvise their own sound sequences.

## DANCE DEVELOPMENT

- Choose one of the children to play an improvised cymbal sequence for the other children to respond to individually in movement.
- Give other children the opportunity to lead the dancers.

## PERFORMANCE

- Group the children in pairs, each with a set of cymbals. One child plays an improvised sequence of sounds on the cymbals while their partner moves in response.
- Encourage the musician to guide the dancer's spatial position, eg
  - by playing near the floor or high in the air;
  - by standing still or travelling in the space;
  - guiding them backwards and forwards.

# STICK TRICKS

**Stick tricks** is performed to the music of the **Saek pole dance** from Thailand, in which musicians sit on the ground in facing pairs to play rhythms on long wooden sticks. Dancers compete to step nimbly over the sticks as the tempo gradually increases.

## Dance objectives

- Use basic dance actions of travelling and jumping within the context of a cultural game idea.
- Maintain a rhythm using props and maintain a stepping pattern.
- Work in small groups.

## Music objectives

- Keep a steady beat, responding to gradual changes of tempo.
- Perform a rhythmic pattern played in pairs on sticks.

## Resources

- Claves or home-made sticks.

## Preparation

Make a pair of newspaper sticks for each child. Tightly roll up four or five complete sheets of newspaper or magazine to make 'sticks', about 18cm long (A broadsheet can be cut into three). Secure the rolls with tape. Decorate by painting them or covering with sticky-back plastic.

Tell the children about the Thai dance-game called the saek pole dance, which is illustrated opposite. Parallel pairs of poles are clashed together rhythmically, while dancers perform steps between them, avoiding catching their ankles as the poles are clashed together faster and faster.

# MUSIC EXPLORATION

## ⑰ CAN YOU KEEP THE BEAT WITH ME?

Each child holds a pair of newspaper sticks. Play a steady beat on a tambour or small drum as you chant (reference track 17):

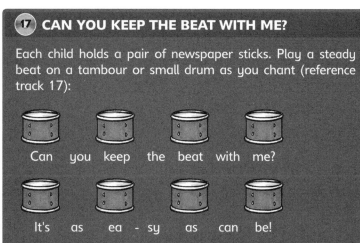

Can you keep the beat with me?

It's as ea - sy as can be!

Invite the children to tap their sticks together to match the beat as you continue playing at the end of the chant.

Choose a child to be leader, saying the chant and setting a steady beat on the drum for the class to match.

## ⑱ TEMPO TRICKS

Now play the drum as you chant (reference track 18):

Keep the beat to match my speed

Ears and sticks are all you need!

The class join in, tapping the beat with you and matching the tempo of your beat as you gradually change it – speeding up or slowing down.

Choose a child to be leader, reminding them that they will need to change speed gradually (not suddenly) and not become too fast, so that the class can stay together.

# DANCE EXPLORATION

• To support the children with listening and moving on the beat, ask the children to tap their knees in time as you say this chant and tap a steady beat on a small hand drum:

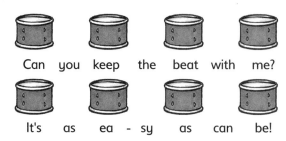

Can you keep the beat with me?

It's as ea - sy as can be!

• Transfer the beat from knees to feet, stepping L to R on the spot in time with the drum beat.

• Now ask them to walk to the beat of the chant and drum, following their own individual paths and using the whole space.

• Develop this into different actions on the beat, eg jogging, jumping, hopping, hopscotching (keeping the feet moving neatly on the beat).

• Develop this further with this chant, changing the tempo of the drum beat you play, speeding up, slowing down, staying the same, etc:

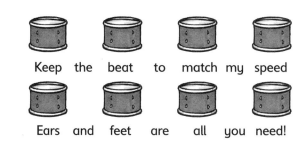

Keep the beat to match my speed

Ears and feet are all you need!

## ⑲ SAEK POLE DANCE

As they listen to the music, the children join in by tapping the rhythm of the poles on their knees and hands:

knees knees clap        knees knees clap...

- Combine the movements:

  – half the children stand in their own space, performing the rhythm of the poles on knees and hands;

  – half the children travel around the space and the standing children, using their own choice of travelling movement on the beat:

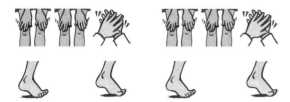

## MUSIC DEVELOPMENT

- Divide the children into pairs, each with two sticks. Sit all the children cross-legged on the floor in rows, facing their partners.

- Say and clap this chant together:

Tap    tap    up        tap    tap    down ...

then learn this tapping pattern, using the sticks:

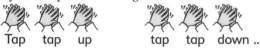

tog    tog    R        tog    tog    L ...

(tog – tap own sticks together; R – tap right sticks with partner; L – tap left sticks with partner.)

- Play a steady drum beat as the children practise the tapping pattern and say the chant.

- When they are confident encourage them to say the chant in their heads.

- Choose a leader to play the drum at a steady beat while you or another child say the chant, Can you keep the beat with me? The stick players join in with their pattern at the end of the chant:

- Chant *Tempo tricks*, and begin altering the tempo as the stick players join in. Let individuals be leader, choosing their own tempo changes.

- Encourage pairs of children to make up their own stick patterns to play both versions of the game.

## DANCE DEVELOPMENT

- Begin to work with sticks and movement linked together.

- Introduce 'tap tap up, tap tap down'. Do this initially on the spot, and then progress to travelling forwards on 'tap tap up', back on 'tap tap down'.

- Develop this further by working with a partner. Begin apart and take two steps forwards and touch sticks together high, take two steps backwards (away from each other), and touch the floor with the stick.

- Once the pairs have established this pattern, put the pairs into facing line formations:

X        X

X        X

X        X

X        X

X        X

Can the formation work in unison with sticks and movements?

- As the children become skilful with this rhythm, begin to speed it up.

- Develop the activity into a game in which individual children choose a way to travel from one end of the facing lines of stick players to the other, eg jumping, walking, skipping. The dancers need to choose their moment carefully to avoid the pairs of sticks as they clash together.

## PERFORMANCE

- Pairs of children or small groups create their own stick dance and combine them with new stick-tapping patterns, eg tap both sticks on floor, then in the air for a silent beat, swap places and repeat.

- Encourage the children to create new rhythms with the sticks and be inventive with the accompanying dance movements in order to find their own new stick tricks.

# TIME LINE

*Time line* is based on a piece of Italian Renaissance dance music by Giorgio Mainerio called *Schiarazula marazula* which features a simple, repeating melody and hand clapping pattern.

## Dance objectives
- Work with a rhythmic pattern.
- Develop patterns using relationships and space.

## Music objectives
- Explore rhythm patterns (ostinato) using body percussion and untuned percussion.
- Perform in groups to combine a melody with a rhythmic ostinato.

## Resources
– drum and claves
– kazoo

## Preparation
Ensure that you know the patterns yourself.

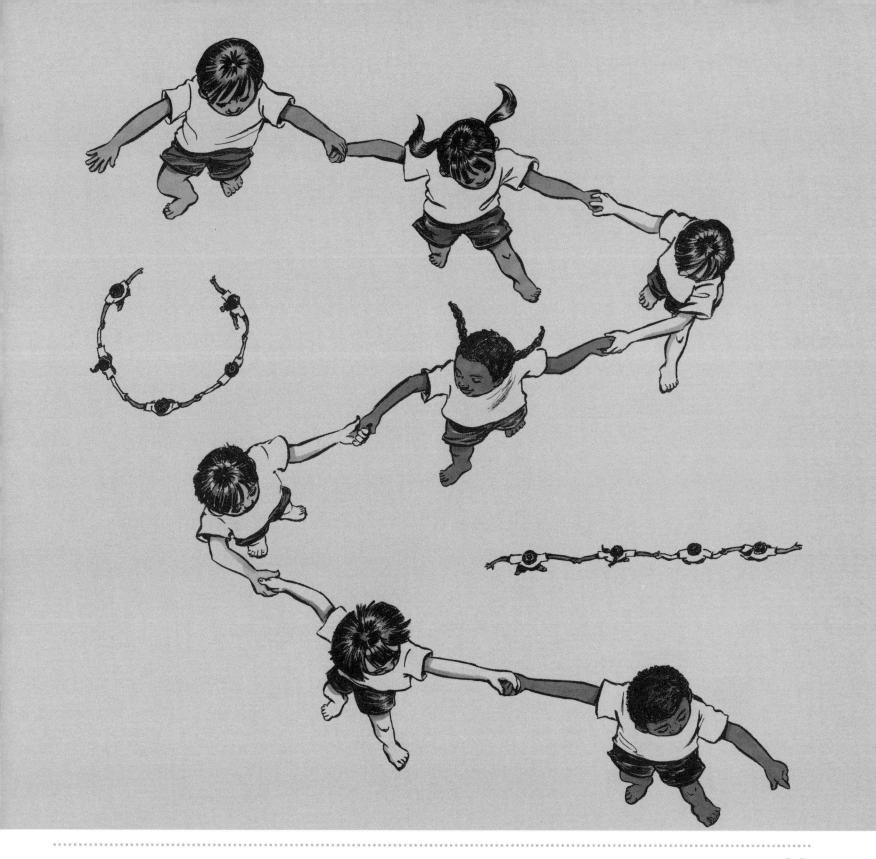

## 20 ONE TWO CLAP CLAP CLAP

As you all listen to the music, join in with the hand claps.

Ask the children how many claps there are in each pattern. (Three.)

As you listen again, explore ways suggested by the children for marking beats one and two with body percussion between the hand claps through beats 3 and 4, eg:

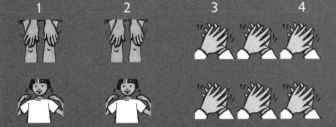

Divide into two groups to explore the patterns further:

Group 1                    Group 2

Swap patterns so that all the children have a chance to play the clapping pattern.

## 21 SCHIARAZULA MARAZULA

As in the music exploration, join in with the handclapping as you all listen to the CD.

Ask the children to stand in their own personal space and transfer the handclapping rhythm to different parts of the body – shoulders, hands, knees, feet:

| 1 | 2 | 3 | 4 |

Still standing in their own space, the children add left and right foot stamps on the handclapping rhythm:

| 1 | 2 | 3 | 4 |

L    R    L

On the next group of four beats this becomes:

| 1 | 2 | 3 | 4 |

R    L    R

Perform this foot pattern as the music plays. Some children may find it helpful to perform the handclapping at the same time, others will find it easier to concentrate just on feet.

# MUSIC DEVELOPMENT

 **22-23 ZARALAZOO**

Listen to track 22 to learn melody A. Sing along with the melody to 'doo'.

Now learn melody B (track 23), again singing along to 'doo'.

All hum the whole melody four times while a small group of children play it on kazoos:

A A B B x 4

Select another small group of children to accompany the melody by playing the beat on drum and the clapping rhythm on claves as in the recording (track 20):

| 1 | 2 | 3 | 4 |

**21/24 ZARALAZOO**

Still in groups, the children follow their leaders in and around the space creating different floor patterns as track 24 plays.

Introduce the children to a swivel turn: this is performed by a line of children swivelling 180° to face the opposite direction. The child at the end of the line becomes the new leader. The children may find this coordinated turn easier to perform if they join hands (still facing forward).

Practise this with track 24 on which a caller signals the swivel turn at the end of the A and B melodies. The new leader continues the pattern in one direction until the melody changes, and the caller signals the line to swivel again.

Practise with the sample track until the children have mastered the coordination of this tricky turn.

# DANCE DEVELOPMENT

- Standing in their own personal space ask the children to revise the stamping pattern they learnt in the exploration while you or a child perform the drum and claves accompaniment:

        L(R)    R(L)    L(R) ...

- When this is established, ask the children to move forward by stepping, jumping or jogging on the drum beat:

  step        step        L(R)    R(L)    L(R) ...

- When the children can perform this in a straight line, encourage them to use different pathways, eg curved lines, zig zags.

- To develop the work further, put the children in groups of four to six with a leader. The groups follow their leaders' path and choice of movement, jogging or stepping. Everyone stamps on the handclap rhythm.

# PERFORMANCE

- Perform the line dance in small groups deciding beforehand whether to

  – use the children's own percussion and kazoo accompaniment (decide upon the number of times to repeat the melodies);

  – use the called Zaralazoo track (24);

  – use Schiarazula marazula (21);

  – join hands in a line;

  – change steps or keep them the same.

# WALK THE WALK

*Bushido Part 2* is by ekstrak and was inspired by the movements and emotions of a samurai. It was composed using a variety of computer programmes; Cubase SX for all sequencing: OSCar synth for the four bass lines: and a combination of phonographic 'found sound' along with editing in Sound Forge to produce the sound ingredients.

## Dance objectives

- Use contrasting qualities of movement in different sections of a dance.
- Work in unison in small groups.
- Link actions fluently together.

## Music objectives

- Explore beat and rhythm by using the voice to perform strongly rhythmic chants linked to sequences of physical movement.
- Perform strongly rhythmic chants, adding vocal sound patterns.

## Preparation

Show the children the videoclip of the dancer, Leon Hazlewood, improvising the steps from which their own dance work will be devised.

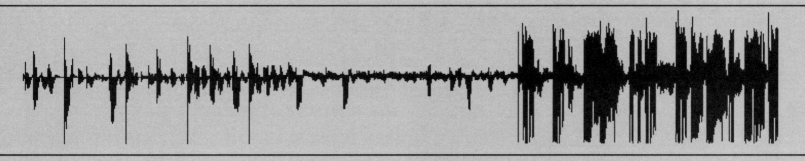

# DANCE EXPLORATION

- Using tracks 25-28 (in which the 8 x 8 beats are counted), teach the children these four different movement patterns, which are all associated with an urban journey.

### 25 AT THE BUS STOP 8 x 8 counts

1-4: fold arms and tap right foot four times;

5: look to the right; 6: look to the left;

7-8: look at watch on left arm. (Repeat all x 8.)

### 26 WALKING DOWN THE STREET 8 x 8 counts

1-4: walk forward for four steps;

5-6: walk backwards for two steps;

7-8: swivel round and walk forwards for two steps. (Change direction and repeat all x 8.)

### 27 LIFT GOING DOWN 8 x 8 counts

Raise hands in front of face, palms facing inward.

1: open hands;

2-3: step forward on right foot, close left foot up;

4: close hands;

5-6: bend knees;

7-8: stretch knees. (Repeat all x 8.)

### 28 IN THE TUBE 8 x 8 counts

1-2: step in sideways on right foot, close left foot up;

3-4: sit down;

5-6: stand and reach up for tube strap;

7-8: jiggle and wriggle. (Repeat all x 8.)

# MUSIC EXPLORATION

- Remind the children of the four types of transport referred to in the music: waiting at the bus stop, walking, underground station lift, underground train.

### 29 BUSHIDO PART 2

As they listen to the music, the children signal the start of each of the four main sound patterns, eg they hail a bus, walk their arms, mime lift doors opening and closing, mime holding a tube train strap.

### 30/31 TALK THE TALK

Teach the children the *Talk the talk* chants (track 30):

AT THE BUS STOP section 1

Waitin' in the queue for a number 8.
Where's that bus? It's makin' me late.

WALKING DOWN THE STREET section 2

Walk down the city street,
Backstep, turn on the beat.

LIFT GOING DOWN section 3

Lift doors open, in we go,
Doors close, down below.

IN THE TUBE section 4

Mind the gap! Sit down!
Hold tight! Hang on the strap!

Use backing track 31 to practise saying the chants in unison and in time to the beat. Change to each new chant as its matching pattern is heard in the music:

| x8 | x8 | x8 | x8 |
|---|---|---|---|
|  |  |  |  |

Perform the chants with tracks 25-28, then track 29.

## DANCE DEVELOPMENT

- Divide into four groups, and give each group time to rehearse the four movement patterns along with track 29.

- When the groups are confident, perform the dance as a round: group 1 starts at the bus stop and continues their journey; when this first group reach the walking down the street pattern, group 2 starts at the bus stop. Continue until all the groups are moving through the patterns from the beginning to the end (the last group will perform only the first pattern).

## MUSIC DEVELOPMENT

- Divide the class into four groups. Give each group time to rehearse the four chants to track 29.

- Ask each group to contribute their own word patterns to add to the chants, eg beatbox rhythms (dum__ dum-dum, dum___ dum-dum, or p p ch__p p ch__ ). Combine these with the chants.

- When all the groups can confidently perform the chants along with track 29 and with their added vocal sound patterns, perform *Talk the talk* as a round. This time each group begins in turn and continues to the end of the music (track 29). Group 2 begins when Group 1 reaches the second chant, and so on until all the groups are in (group 4 will only perform the first chant).

## PERFORMANCE

- In the groups from the development, the children decide whether to be dancers or chanters. Combine the movement patterns and chants and beatbox rhythms with the CD. Perform the complete work as a round.

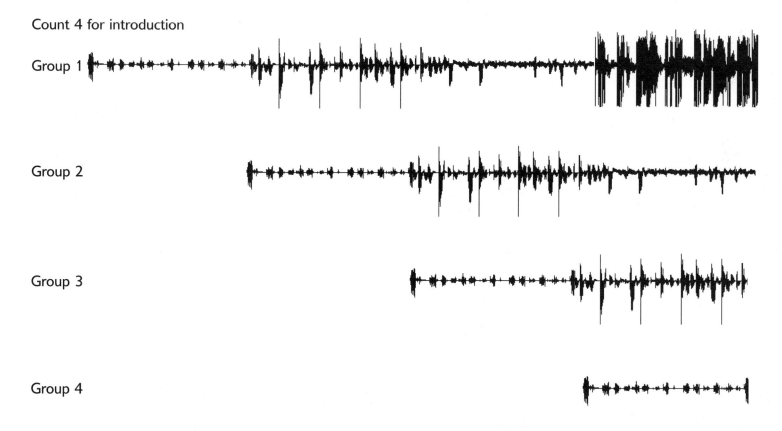

Count 4 for introduction

Group 1

Group 2

Group 3

Group 4

# DRAGON HUNT

***In the Hall of the Mountain King*** comes from the Peer Gynt Suite of orchestral music by Edvard Grieg. There are three sections, which gradually increase in tempo and build in excitement as more instruments join in.

## Dance objectives

- Use contrasting levels and directions.
- Choose appropriate movement and dynamics to interpret a story.
- Work in pairs and small groups.
- Perform a whole dance with a simple structure.

## Music objectives

- Perform a simple arrangement of a song, including a two-note ostinato and rhythmic percussion accompaniment.
- Perform changes in tempo.
- Compose musical interludes in response to the stimuli of different environments.
- Compose a musical ending.

## Resources

- Enlarged copy of the map.
- Tuned percussion notes D and A (the lowest sounding you have).
- Selection of percussion.

## Preparation

Show the children the map opposite. Ask them what they think is going to happen (three children go on a dragon hunt). Encourage the children to describe the obstacles which the explorers meet on the way and to use their imagination to describe the events. They need to discuss the different endings which the story might have, eg the dragon wakes up and scares them away, they scare the dragon, they make friends, they run back through all the obstacles.

Tangly forest

##  **32** IN THE HALL OF THE MOUNTAIN KING

With their eyes closed, the children listen to the music and imagine the journey to find the dragon:

– what can they see?

– how does it make them feel?

– how does the journey end? (The dragon wakes up, they all freeze, they run quickly away, they hide...)

##  **33** THE DRAGON HUNT MARCH

Explore stepping patterns in and around the space, using the music as an accompaniment, eg

> walking backwards/forwards
>
> galloping sideways
>
> skipping forwards and backwards
>
> hopscotching in a circle

In twos or threes, the children choose some travelling steps which they can remember and repeat to the accompaniment of the music.

## **34** THE DRAGON HUNT MARCH (GETTING FASTER)

Listen to track 34. What do the children notice? (The chant speeds up each time it is repeated.)

Can the children perform their travelling patterns, matching the changes in the tempo of the chant?

Can they travel one behind the other?

## **33** THE DRAGON HUNT MARCH

Listen to the CD (track 33) to learn *The Dragon Hunt March* which can be chanted or sung.

We're going on a dragon hunt, dragon hunt, dragon hunt

We're going on a dragon hunt to find a dragon's lair!

*(Repeat)*

Choose one or two players to add tuned percussion (the lowest you have, notes D and A). Make sure that the players and chanters can keep a steady beat. Practise with the CD at first, then try without.

Going on a dragon hunt, dragon hunt, dragon hunt...

Add a few small hand-held percussion instruments, eg egg shakers, claves, and ask the players to accompany the chant by playing the rhythm of the words.

Go-ing on a dra-gon hunt, dra-gon hunt, dra-gon hunt...

##  **34** THE DRAGON HUNT MARCH (GETTING FASTER)

Listen to track 34. What do the children notice? (The chant speeds up each time it is repeated)

Perform the chant or song with the CD, using rhythm percussion and the ostinato, matching the changes in tempo.

## **32** IN THE HALL OF THE MOUNTAIN KING

Now listen to Grieg's music again. What do the children recognise? ( The music starts slowly and becomes gradually faster, louder and more exciting. The melody is the same as the one played with the chant.)

What happens musically at the end of the story? (The music becomes even louder and faster)

Ask the children how they think the story ends, eg the dragon wakes up, the children run away ...

## DANCE DEVELOPMENT

- Using the map as a guide, begin to take the children on the dragon hunt, and find ways in twos and threes to encounter the hazards:

**Tangly forest** – over, under, around and between, using different actions to explore these spatial elements eg stretching, bending, twisting, turning, sliding, rolling and jumping.

(*Qualities* – ABANDONED, FLEXIBLE, STRONG, UNDULATING movement.)

**Swamp** – through swamp using pulling, stretching movements.

(*Qualities* – HEAVY, LOW, STRONG, DRAGGING movement.)

**Stepping stones** – onto and across the stone using a variety of jumping actions and large steps/small steps.

(*Qualities* – LIGHT, DIRECT, BOUNDING, BOUNCY movement.)

**Rope bridge** – across and along the rope using very careful and controlled steps and/or hands and feet

(*Qualities* – CONTROLLED, LIGHT, CAREFUL, DIRECT, SLOW movement.)

**Canoe lake** – across the lake using paddling actions in unison, one behind the other. Experiment with using different levels and travelling actions, ie row and slide or row and step

(*Qualities* – FIRM, STRONG, RHYTHMIC, SMOOTH movement.)

**Mountain tunnel** – under and through the tunnel using low travelling actions – slide, roll, creep, crawl, push, pull.

(*Qualities* – DIRECT, FIRM, STRONG, SMOOTH, CONTROLLED movement.)

## MUSIC DEVELOPMENT

- Show the children the map which leads to the dragon's cave, asking them to describe the hazards they will meet on the journey:

| | | |
|---|---|---|
| **Tangly forest** | **Swamp** | **Stepping stone river** |
| **Rope bridge** | **Canoe lake** | **Mountain tunnel** |

- Together choose a sound or sounds to represent each of the hazards, eg

**Tangly forest** – pieces of plastic wrapping rubbed together;

**Swamp** – water sloshed in plastic bottle;

**Stepping stones** – random individual notes played on xylophone;

**Rope bridge** – two beaters 'rolling' (played alternate LRLR) on single chimebar or xylophone;

**Canoe lake** – beaters sliding up and down glockenspiel;

**Mountain tunnel** – low humming into large cardboard tube.

- Choose a conductor to point to the route on the map as a chosen group of players perform their sounds for each hazard. The same group of players perform the chant in between each of the hazards, starting very slowly and quietly, then getting gradually louder and faster with each repetition.

## PERFORMANCE

- Perform the story without the CD, organising the hazard sounds, the chant and dance to tell the story. To complete the performance, the musicians and dancers decide how to end the story and decide how to accompany the ending musically. The dancers will respond improvisationally in movement. Appoint:

**a conductor** to indicate the finish;

**musicians** to perform hazard sounds, the chant and an ending;

**dancers** to perform stepping patterns, hazard actions, and ending movements in twos or threes.

# PULA

*Pula* is music from the Qwii, 'the first people', of Southern Africa. In the ancient traditions of these nomadic hunter gatherers music is used to celebrate and mark the passing of all stages in life. *Pula* is a song of praise to the rain, sustainer of life. The dance developed here moves out of the context of Qwii tradition into a celebration of the planting, growing and harvesting of maize.

## Dance objectives
- Observe and identify working actions, and characteristics of African dance.
- Perform working actions rhythmically, showing control and co-ordination.
- Use characteristics from African dance to enhance a performance.

## Music objectives
- Create descriptive sounds which represent rainfall.
- Perform a piece of music which combines rhythm, melodic ostinato and voices.
- Create an arrangement.

## Resources
- Tuned percussion and/or keyboard notes.
- Maracas, cabasas, shakers.
- Video recorder.

## Preparation
Show the children the videoclip of a dance interpretation of *Pula*, showing the cycle of growing food and preparing it to share. Talk about the actions the dancer performs: an opening depiction of rain followed by strongly rhythmic actions – digging, planting, cutting, collecting, celebrating, pounding grain, stirring, patting maize cakes, sharing the good food.

# DANCE EXPLORATION

##  35 RAIN MUSIC

As the children listen to this short piece of rain music, they improvise movements to show rainfall, eg

– stretching hands high with fingertips wiggling down, tickling over the face, chest, tummy, thighs and knees towards the floor.

Look for good movements to share with each other. When everyone has some movements established, perform them again to the music.

• The children know from their preparation that the rain which has fallen will help the crops to grow and be harvested. Remind the children of the working actions they saw performed on the videoclip:

| | |
|---|---|
| digging | pounding grain |
| planting | stirring |
| cutting | patting dough |
| collecting | sharing |

## 36 PULA – WORKING ACTIONS

Encourage the children to perform the work actions rhythmically with the music of **Pula**.

The actions are repeated and performed using both sides of the body. Begin to introduce travelling.

Try to improve the performance style of these actions by encouraging the children to bend their knees and keep the actions low to the ground whilst maintaining a strong upper body – always keeping it rhythmical.

## 37 PULA CALL AND RESPONSE CELEBRATION

Ask the children to respond to the call 'pula' by making large, open, stretched shapes whilst calling 'ayene' to express the idea of joy at the gathering of the harvest.

# MUSIC EXPLORATION

##  38 PULA

Listen to the music, explaining the background (see preparation). Invite the children to clap the beat as they listen.

### Rain sounds

• Make a set of rainmakers, using:

a variety of cardboard tubes, plastic tubs, flat chocolate boxes, lengths of corrugated hose containing grains, rice, lentils, gravel; or collect together a variety of shakers.

• Explore ways of playing the rainmakers to make rain sounds. Try:

gently shaking in the air to make long sounds;

swirling in circles;

gently tipping from one end to the other;

rolling cylindrical or spherical instruments between the palms of both hands.

## 39-40 WORK MUSIC – XYLOPHONE

Listen to the xylophone on track 39 playing this pattern. Invite one or two players to learn it:

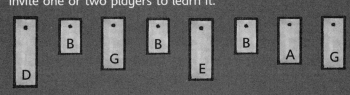

When the xylophone players are confident, invite the rest of the class to join in by clapping the beat. Choose a small group to add shakers, tapping the instruments gently in the palm of the hand to keep a fast steady beat, track 40:

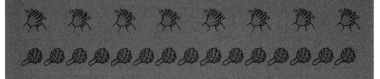

- Perform the work music using this structure:

  xylophones play their pattern once with hand claps on the beat;

  shakers join in – repeat xylophone pattern once more;

  all play as many times as liked.

## 41 CALL AND RESPONSE – CELEBRATION

Use track 41 to learn the 'pula - ayene' call and response. The children respond to the caller's 'pula' with the response, 'ayene'.

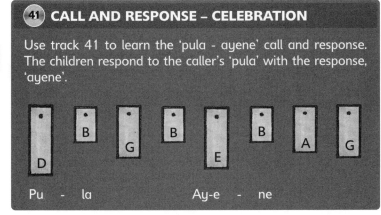

Pu - la          Ay-e - ne

- Practise without the CD, first giving the children the call yourself, then inviting individuals to take turns to be the caller.

- Perform the call and response with the work music.

# DANCE DEVELOPMENT

## 35-38 PULA

Link the first and second sections together, so that children can show the story through their movement:

- Rainfall;

- Working and celebrating actions.

(The class might be split into three groups to perform the three types of action: rainfall, working and celebrating.)

# MUSIC DEVELOPMENT

### Rain sounds

- Decide how to organise or combine the rain sounds to make a piece of rain music. You might:

  **play individual instruments in turn**, overlapping each sound;

  **layer the sounds**, starting one by one until all are playing, then dropping out one by one;

  **all play together**, starting quietly, then gradually increasing the volume.

- Make a picture or graphic score of your rain music to show how it is organised.

### Work music

- Invite individuals to improvise rhythms on drums to accompany the xylophone pattern and shaker during the work music.

### Call and response – celebration

- Together, decide when to add the call and response to the work music, and how many times it will be repeated. Draw or write a plan of the piece in your chosen order. Rehearse the whole structure and choose an ending for the piece, eg all call out 'PULA!'

# PERFORMANCE

- Decide on a matching structure for the dance and music, eg how many times you will repeat the work music, when you will add the call and response and how many times it will be repeated.

- Rehearse the music and dance together, using a video recorder to help the children assess any necessary improvements.

- Rehearse your chosen ending. Perform to an audience.

## Shoolie-Shoo

Just from the kit-chen,_ shoo-lie - shoo,_ With a hand-ful of cook-ies,_ shoo-lie - shoo,_ O,_

_ dear Da - niel, shoo-lie - shoo,_ Fly a-way o-ver yon-der, shoo-lie - shoo._

## The grasshopper's song

Can you dance, can you dance, can you reel? Can you dance, can you dance, can you

click your heels? Can you dance all night long at the in - sect ball, Do the grass-hop-per's dance with me!

## We're going on a dragon hunt

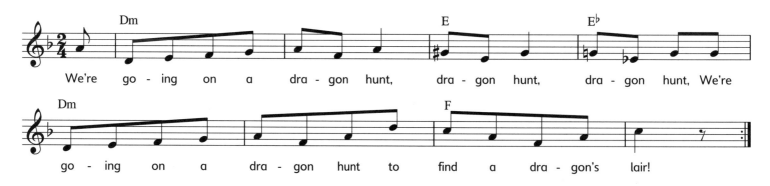

We're go - ing on a dra - gon hunt, dra - gon hunt, dra - gon hunt, We're

go - ing on a dra - gon hunt to find a dra - gon's lair!

# ACKNOWLEDGEMENTS

The following copyright holders have kindly given their permission for the inclusion of their copyright material in this book and CD pack.

Every effort has been made to trace and acknowledge copyright owners. If any right has been omitted, the publishers offer their apologies and will rectify this in subsequent editions following notification.

**All rights of the producer and of the owner of the works reproduced reserved. Unauthorised copying, hiring, lending, public performance and broadcasting of the text, recordings and videoclips prohibited.**

## AUDIO TRACKS

**Schiarazula marazula**
Performed by Ulsamer Collegium, conducted by Josef Ulsamer. Used courtesy of Deutsche Grammophon part of the Universal Music Group.

**Jelly Roll Blues**
By Louis Armstrong, Paul Rodriguez Music on Prestige Elite Records 1994 Jazz Veterans for Sunday Times. Used by permission. All Rights Reserved.

**In the Hall of the Mountain King**
From Peer Gynt Suite No 1 Opus 46:4 In the Hall of the Mountain King. Performed by The English Chamber Orchestra, conducted by Raymond Leppard. Courtesy of Phillips Classics. Licensed by The Film & TV Licensing Division, part of the Universal Music Group.

**Sorbet No 2.**
By Evelyn Glennie. Licensed by BMG UK & Ireland Ltd on behalf of BMG. Taken from the album 'Drumming' on the BMG Catalyst Label 09026 68195 2.

**The Grasshopper's Dance**
By Ernest Bucalossi from the album British Light Music Classics performed by The New London Orchestra, conducted by Ronald Corp CDA66968. Used by permission of Hyperion Records Ltd.

**Sumer is icumen in**
By Robert Saxton from Variations on Sumer is icumen in, Themes and Variations performed by the BBC Symphony Orchestra, conducted by Jac Van Steen (NMC D062) © 2001 NMC Recordings Ltd.

**Pula**
From Bushmen: Qwii – The First People, ARC EUCD 1553. With kind permission of ARC Music Productions International Ltd ℗ & © 2002.

**Jarabe Tapatio**
Performed by Mariachi Sol taken from Cu-cu-rru-cu-cu, Paloma ARC EUCD 1246. With kind permission of ARC Music Productions International Ltd ℗ & © 2002.

**Saek Pole Dance**
From Music from Thailand and Laos ARC EUCD 1425. With kind permission of ARC Music Productions International Ltd ℗ & © 2002.

**Sounds Menu**
By Stephen Chadwick © 2002, from Music Express Year 1, A&C Black Publishers Ltd.

**Bushido Part 2**
By ekstrak, remastered for Walk the walk © 2003, A&C Black Publishers Ltd.

All other tracks performed by Debbie Sanders (voice) and Stephen Chadwick. Recorded for A&C Black Publishers Ltd, © 2003.

## VIDEOCLIPS

**Underwater world** and **Twister**
Footage supplied under licence by Moving Image, 61 Great Titchfield Street, London W1, www.milibrary.com. Used by permission.

All other videoclips filmed and produced by Jamie Acton-Bond for A&C Black Publishers Ltd. Activities by Bobbie Gargrave and Helen MacGregor. Additional performances by Leon Hazlewood, and dance students Aran, Lisa and Temmi of Dagenham Priory School.
The authors and publishers extend special thanks to the staff and pupils of the schools involved in filming the videoclips:
Jo Fitzmaurice, Gloucester Primary, Peckham;
Mr J Sims and Samantha James, St Josephs Primary School, Barking;
Susie Davison, Amy Probert, Miss Kaye, Christine Newcombe, and Miss Evans, Marsh Green Primary School, Dagenham.

Thanks are also due to the London Boroughs of Barking and Dagenham, and Southwark.

# MORE MUSIC AND DANCE FROM A&C BLACK

## LET'S GO ZUDIE-O

The award winning companion title to Let's go shoolie-shoo for children in the early years. Twelve units of stimulating and enjoyable dance and music activities based on music from around the world and from different historical times. **No music reading required.**
ISBN 0-7136-5489-9

## MUSIC EXPRESS

This complete music scheme for practitioners and teachers of children aged 3 to 11 won the Education Resources Award for Best Primary Resource 2003. It is an outstanding series for general class teachers, which offers complete planning and activities for music lessons. **No music reading required.**
FS ISBN 0-7136-6582-3
Y1 ISBN 0-7136-6231-X
Y2 ISBN 0-7136-6227-1
Y3 ISBN 0-7136-6229-8
Y4 ISBN 0-7136-6232-8
Y5 ISBN 0-7136-6228-X
Y6 ISBN 0-7136-6230-1

## LISTENING TO MUSIC AGE 5+

Accessible, stimulating ways into listening to music, involving active participation. Music chosen from different historical times and from across the world. **No music reading required.**
ISBN 0-7136-4173-8

## BOBBY SHAFTOE CLAP YOUR HANDS

Favourite children's melodies with new words and activities to explore basic skills in music. **No music reading required.**
ISBN 0-7136-3556-8

## THREE SINGING PIGS

A collection of traditional and new stories each containing a song, a rap or a chant. A wonderful resource of musical activities for performing, listening and composing. **No music reading required.**
ISBN 0-7136-3804-4

**For a full list of titles, including music for the classroom, song books, musicals, CDs and cassettes, assembly resources and instrumental tutors, contact:**

**A&C Black, PO Box 19, St Neots, Cambs PE19 8SF
Telephone: 01480 212666 Fax: 01480 405014
e-mail: sales@acblack.com**

## WWW.ACBLACK.COM